THE LITTLE SNOWMAN

Design: Diane Stevenson / Snap Haus Graphics

THE LITTLE SNOWMAN

Sheila Black

Illustrated by Paul Selwyn

Ariel Books • Andrews and McMeel • Kansas City

"The first snow of the year and our sled is broken," sighed Billy, looking around the snow-covered yard.

"I know," his sister, Amanda, said. "And the Perrys are away, so we can't even have a good snowball fight."

"You could build a snowman," suggested their grandfather.

"Our snowmen never come out right," said Amanda.

"I'll show you how to do it," Grandfather replied. "I built a snowman every year until I was grown up almost. In fact, I have the buttons I always used for his eyes right here." Grandfather reached into his pocket and pulled out two big, shiny, blue buttons.

Crunch, crunch went the snow under the children's mittens. "Perfect sledding snow," said Billy. "Perfect snowball snow," said Amanda.

It turned out to be perfect snowman snow, too. In no time at all they had two big round balls patted and smoothed into shape on the snowy lawn. Grandfather went back inside, and Billy went with him to pick out a hat and mittens for their snowman. The hat and mittens fit perfectly! Billy wrapped his own scarf 'round the snowman's neck. Amanda put Grandfather's buttons where his eyes should be. "There!" she cried. "Doesn't he look nice?"

"Not bad," Billy said.

"Not bad?" said a voice. It was a funny voice, almost like the crunch, crunch of snow. "I think I look SPLENDID!"

The children gaped in wonder. Their snowman could talk! "But . . . you're alive!" shouted Billy.

"Of course I'm alive," the snowman replied.

"But snowmen aren't supposed to be alive," said Amanda.

"And they're not supposed to talk, either," put in Billy.

"They do where I come from."

"And where is that?" both children demanded.

"Why, SNOWLAND of course."

"Snowland?"

"Yes, Snowland. Would you like to go there?"

Billy and Amanda looked at each other. "Don't worry," the snowman said. "It's perfectly safe. Here, each of you take an arm, and off we'll go!" Billy took hold of one round arm, and Amanda took the other. Snowflakes fell around them so thickly they couldn't see their mittens in front of their faces.

When the snowflakes cleared, the children were standing in the middle of a beautiful frozen lake. Snowy mountains gleamed in the distance. All around candy-colored penguins frolicked about. Some had sleds, some had skates, and some were sailing across the ice.

"Hooray!" cried Billy. "Can we play with them?"

"Oh, yes!" said the snowman. "*I* plan to!" So the three of them happily whizzed and slid about with the penguins, until the snowman said they must be on their way. "We've still got to get to Snowtown," he explained.

They walked on past a frozen seashore, where huge icebergs floated. On one of them sat a pair of giant polar bears. The polar bears waved and called out, "Hello, there!" in their gruff bear voices. Billy and Amanda longed to stop, but the little snowman rushed them on.

"Look, there's Snowtown!" Amanda shouted. What a pretty place it was! The buildings were all carved out of snow and ice. Colorful flags flew from glistening towers. Billy ran on ahead and tumbled headfirst into the snow. "Come on," he said. "Let's go!"

At the Snowtown harbor, walruses and seals splashed about in the icy water. "Hello, how do you do!" they barked, bobbing up to shake flippers with Billy and Amanda.

In the center of town, smiling snowmen and snowwomen bustled down the glittering streets. Everywhere you looked, roly-poly snow children were lobbing snowballs back and forth.

"Can't we please play with them?" Amanda begged. The little snowman nodded. Soon they were ducking and dodging, tossing snowballs every which way.

They had so much fun they hoped it would never end. But the snowman declared it was time for a snack. He led them to his own neat little snow house. A jolly round snow lady was waiting for them there. "I've just made a fresh batch of snow cones," she said. "Go on. Eat them while they're cold!"

The snow cones tasted like ice cream, frozen custard, Popsicles, and every other delicious cold thing you can imagine. Billy and Amanda ate and ate.

Suddenly, Amanda's toes began to tingle. Billy realized he couldn't even feel the tip of his nose. The snowman peered down at them. "Dear me," he said. "You two are quite blue with cold. I think we better get you home."

The little snowman politely gave Amanda one arm and Billy the other. Snowflakes whirled around them so thickly they had to close their eyes.

When they opened them again, they were back in their own front yard. And the snowman was standing there, very stiff and still.

The door of their house opened. "You two have been playing long enough," their mother called out. "Come in. I've made you hot cocoa with marshmallows." Billy and Amanda hesitated. But then they heard the snowman whisper, "Go on, children. Don't worry. I'll see you —" The last word was too faint for them to hear, but it sounded like "tomorrow."

That night Billy and Amanda dreamed of Snowland and of all the marvelous things they had seen there. They woke up excited, ready to go out and play with the little snowman again. But then Billy noticed a drip-drip sound. Amanda looked out the window and gave a cry of dismay.

The sun was shining, and the snow was melting. Their beautiful snowman was almost all gone. Even his button eyes had been swallowed into a puddle. The children ran to their grandfather. "It isn't fair!" they cried.

"I know," Grandfather sighed. "I was always sad when my snowman melted. But don't worry, your snowman will be back. In the meantime, I have a present for you."

Grandfather pulled a small glass globe out of his pocket. Inside was a tiny snowman. When he shook it, snowflakes whirled down. "It's nice, Grandpa," said Amanda. "But it isn't *our* snowman," said Billy. Suddenly, both children gasped. As they peered at him, the snowman waved one tiny arm. It *was* their snowman! "Goodbye Billy! Goodbye Amanda!" he said in his funny crunchy voice. "See you SOOON!"